Copyright © 2021 by Abby Knox

All rights reserved.

No part of this book may be reproduced in any form or by any electronic or mechanical means, including information storage and retrieval systems, without written permission from the author, except for the use of brief quotations in a book review.

Publisher's Note: This is a work of fiction. Names, characters, places, and incidents are a product of the author's imagination. Locales and public names are sometimes used for atmospheric purposes. Any resemblance to actual people, living or dead, or to businesses, companies, events, institutions, or locales is coincidental.

Edited by Aquila Editing

Cover Designer: Cormar Covers

Elf-napped

A FILTHY DIRTY CHRISTMAS

ABBY KNOX

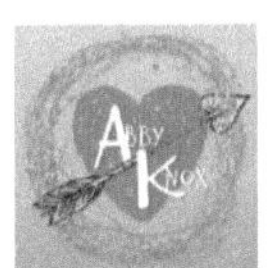

Chapter One

CLARA

Me, texting my friend who convinced me to leave the house today: "This is the worst Tinder date in the history of Tinder dates. I should have stayed home and watched Lord of the Rings again."

Reba doesn't reply right away. She's busy with her long-distance boyfriend Deacon, plus she's totally over my homebody ways.

Earlier, while practically pushing me out the door, Reba had half-joked, "I hate to break it to you, sweetie, But Legolas is never going to be the one to de-virgin you. You have to put yourself out there for the actual human males."

My freezing hand stuffs my phone back in my puffy coat's pocket, and I look up, scanning my surroundings.

What I had hoped might be a casual meet-up for festive fun at the Christmas tree farm has turned out to be a whole mess.

I should be sipping hot cocoa in the farm's faux North

Pole village right now. Perhaps listening to carolers, making a wreath in Santa's Workshop, or browsing ornaments in the gift shop. Holly Berry Farm is a whole experience that people in the city drive their families to on weekends for wholesome fun. And the guy had agreed to my suggestion.

Yet what are we doing instead? Wandering off the farm's property and into the neighboring woods. And why do I not simply let this idiot get lost and freeze to death? Probably because he'd been hitting his flask pretty hard since the moment he arrived, and it's only 11 a.m. He might be an alcoholic, a fact that tugs at my perhaps overly compassionate heart. Dammit.

My tattered thread of hope for a human romantic interest had snapped as soon as I'd smelled Daren's breath upon arrival. "So...you wanna make a wreath and then pick out a tree, or...?" I'd said, determined to make the best of this day now that I had driven 30 minutes out of the city.

I had watched him pour vodka from a flask into a cup of the free apple cider. That should have been my first red flag to turn around and go home.

Did I? No.

Instead, I proceeded to watch my date dash off to hop on the hay wagon, seemingly eager to take the tractor ride out to the tree field right away. "Let's go get us a fuckin' TREE!" He shouted this as if he was an emcee at a wrestling match, and everyone was staring. At me, not him. Because I'm a woman, and I'm supposed to be in charge of a man's behavior?

Fuck my life.

As soon as the tractor approached the field of available trees, Daren bolted off the wagon and wandered off...in the wrong direction.

Right into the Elder Woods. What a dumbass.

I'm not superstitious, but even I know you don't go wandering into the Elder Woods.

"Daren, are you aware that tree shopping involves actually being on the premises of trees that are for sale? And does not entail wandering into the very haunted-looking nearby woods?"

Seems no one is interested in responding to my cries for help today.

Oh, but Daren does utter some vodka-soaked gibberish to himself as we hike deeper and deeper into the woods, farther and farther away from the adorable village.

I'm going to kill Reba. "'Go to Holly Berry Farm,' she said. 'It'll be fun and safe," she said.

I mean, I won't literally kill my best friend. But I intend to remind her as soon as I get home that spending another Saturday afternoon with Orlando Bloom — while wearing my homemade Legolas tee-shirt and swooning at the man's pointy ears and flawless skin — is a much better use of my time than spending a single second with a human man. I lay the blame for my sexual and romantic fixations at the feet of J.R.R. Tolkien and Peter Jackson. One is responsible for my wish to live in a fantasy world, and the other is responsible for the movie that awakened my sexuality.

And now here I am, following this drunk idiot into the woods. Just then, my phone pings.

Reba: "LotR for the 87th time this year is not an option. The fresh air will do you some good."

My parents also thought I needed to get out of the house more. When, as a child, I balked at team sports, they dragged me to martial arts classes. Turns out, I sort of liked those lessons, so I kept going with it to keep my parents happy. It was a pleasant enough trade-off to living the rest of my life with my face in a book.

Me: "Current situation: following his drunk ass into the Elder Woods for god knows what reason."

Reba: "Wut?"

Me: "I should turn around and let him get lost, but I have zero sense of self-preservation despite my martial arts training, evidently."

Reba: ":("

Me: "You and Deacon are walking around the apartment naked, aren't you?"

Reba: "Maybeee?"

Me: "Ugh."

Reba: "We'll get dressed if you decide to come home, I promise."

Honestly, I'm a little surprised that she isn't demanding that I make a 180 and bolt from this date immediately. She may be pushy and slightly manipulative, but she's always looking out for my safety. I can't blame her, though. It's been months since she and Deacon have seen each other. And I'm a black belt in taekwondo. I haven't had to use it on a man yet, and I don't foresee needing to use it to fend off a drunk and sloppy Daren, either.

I look up and see the man trudging through the woods and singing a sea shanty. I've got about 15 pounds on him, and he's a clumsy drunk, so I think I'm okay as far as Daren is concerned. But it's getting colder the deeper we walk into the woods. My sense of kindness is too much for this situation, and I decide I'll have to make sure he doesn't die of exposure out here.

Me: "Nah. I'll herd this cat back to the farm and call a cab for him. Grab me some cocoa and make the most of it. Just... don't go near my Legolas figurines; I don't want his innocent eyes seeing your nakedness."

Reba: "Okay, freak."

Now, where did Daren go? I follow his tracks, muttering that I need therapy to break this habit of being nice to people who exhibit bad behavior.

On the other hand, it is a beautiful walk. I'm enjoying the

cold, crisp air and the sunshine through the bare tree branches. The blanket of snow set against the whispering birches looks like the perfect Christmas postcard. There's even a family of cardinals flying to and fro overhead.

Eventually, the birches give way to a denser collection of massive pines and spruces, their evergreen branches blotting out the sun. I have a growing feeling that we should leave these woods as soon as possible. The Christmas tree farm is about a quarter-mile back, and my feet are numb. And I don't see any branches pointing the way to a lamppost anywhere. God, I spend way too much time with my head in books. This isn't Narnia, Clara.

"Daren!"

"It's up here somewhere," I hear him mutter. "The perfect tree."

I call after him, "We are supposed to be at the farm, making wreaths? Picking an approved tree? Sipping hot cider and cocoa?"

Now I'm just sad and mad.

I should turn back now and never take Reba's advice ever again. She's so caught up in her own romance she forgets to be practical. She threatened to kidnap me and drive me to my date this morning when I was on the verge of canceling.

I had high hopes when I arrived at the farm today. Too bad I didn't stick up for myself. And especially too bad that this adorable North Pole-esque village will never be a place I get to visit with my own children someday.

I just have to face the fact that Legolas isn't real, and I'm never going to have his little elven babies, and I'm going to die a virgin.

Chapter Two

ELDRIN

It's going on five years since I was exiled for loving a human.

To be punished for who I love... doesn't feel very Christmassy and charitable, does it?

The old fat man took everything away. My home, my job, my elven community. Worst of all, he took away my access Clara.

I have watched over her since I grew into my role as List Keeper.

I remember clearly the moment when I fell in love. I was following Clara home from high school, and I saw her walking by the park. A van had pulled up along the curb, and the driver was asking a little boy to help him look for his lost puppy. Clara had sprung into action, put herself between the van and that boy, and told him to run. The driver tried to flee, but Clara performed an incredible nose jab with the heel of her palm. He was incapacitated until the police's arrival. Based on her statements, that man was discovered to be a serial predator and still rots in prison to this day.

That was not only the moment my adolescent brain fell in love with this beautiful human, but also it was the moment I started to question everything. Why were we spying on children and reporting behavior if we couldn't intervene when they were in danger? And why were we surveilling children at all, if not to use our abilities to prevent adults from doing harm?

"Our time would be much better spent making gifts for all children and using our magic to keep adults in check," I told Nicholas during my first performance review.

Nicholas told me to do my job and stop asking questions. That was my first warning.

My second warning was less about my personal sense of right and wrong and a lot more about—well, about my horniness. When Clara turned 18 and had aged out of the Naughty or Nice program, I was supposed to cease my surveillance of her. I was supposed to report to the North Pole and replenish my list with a new batch of children to spy on.

But I never showed up to that meeting. I was too busy watching Clara on a date.

I kept my hawk eyes on her at all times, though unable to prevent her from dating a human. I knew I was in trouble, not meeting my deadlines, not doing my job, but that's what love did to me. I spent all my time feeling frustrated, isolated, and driven mad by jealousy.

And I took advantage of the elven gift of invisibility a few times too many.

One day, Clara went to an outdoor music festival, where she met a man I knew to be bad news. He'd been one of my previous charges, a bad seed. Always on the naughty list and never grew out of it. She'd said no when he put his hands on her. He'd been touching her back, touching her hair. He wouldn't take no for an answer. I waited for my moment, even though I was half-blind with rage. When he wandered off into the trees to relieve himself, I might have encouraged a dying tree to fall on him. He didn't die—I'm not a murderer even though I felt murderous. He walked away with a few broken ribs, and in the meantime, Clara had enough sense to stick close to Reba for the rest of the festival.

Of course, I was caught immediately and brought up on charges of "Interfering in Human Affairs, Causing Bodily Injuries to Humans," and—worst of all in the eyes of Nicholas —"Fixation on an Individual Human."

My punishment? To live out the rest of my days as a caretaker of the Elder Woods.

This is a joke of an assignment.

"Caretaker" means nothing except keeping humans away from our sacred land. Here, the Common elves harvest a unique sap to create healing draughts.

Don't get me wrong, I'm happy that I'm not looking down the barrel of five hundred years of being a List Keeper. I don't give a fuck about exile.

Except for one problem. Nicholas took away my ability to teleport and to be invisible. I'm essentially a very tall human with an ear deformity who will die of extreme old age. For my own survival and the survival of these woods, I can still talk to trees and plants. So at least I have that.

But I can no longer keep my eyes on Clara. I haven't been able to see her in five long years.

Until today.

I've finally got Clara in my sights, by a total fluke of coincidence. And I'm never letting her out of my sight again.

Chapter Three

"THIS IS A TERRIBLE IDEA, DUDE!"

The toasted man is getting us more and more lost, through the dense trees of Elder Woods. And I'm starting to get the creeps.

And then I see the ax.

What the actual fuck?

He turns to face me with a proud grin on his face.

"It's like I said. Cutting down your own Christmas tree used to be a thing that men did all on their own in the woods."

He might have said that in his incoherent rambles, but I hadn't heard it before now. If I had, I'd like to think I would have ditched him miles ago.

This man-boy is certifiable.

I wish whatever creature lives in these woods would pop out and make Daren piss his jeans right now. I'd love for his dick to freeze to them as a result. Not to do any permanent damage, but maybe enough to require medical intervention, like a much more embarrassing version of that scene in *A Christmas Story*.

Daren rounds the corner, and he shouts, "Here it is! This is the one! Fuck yeah!"

"Please do not think about cutting down a tree in these woods!" I exclaim.

Too late. The chopping begins.

Thwack!

"Dude!" I shout. "You do know Clark Griswold is a fictional character, right? You do know this is wrong on so many levels?!"

I hate running. I hate being out of breath. I also hate yelling. The fact that I'm doing all of these things is not lost on me. I'm also going to get caught by the farmer—or whatever weirdo haunts these woods—and be guilty by association.

But my love of natural habitats far outweighs my worry about looking guilty if caught.

Daren doesn't answer but delivers blow after blow to some poor tree. God, just how big is this tree that he's trying to cut down?

"Come on, man! You're being a huge dick right now. Birds probably live in that tree!"

Later in life, when I retell this story to people, I will describe how at this moment, the chopping sounds stopped, and everything seemed to go eerily still.

A human-like shadow cuts across the snow to my right. This is followed by complete and utter silence from the birds and all woodland creatures. Not a single chirp or scuttle can be heard. A minute later, Daren's blood-curdling scream rents the air.

"Daren!?"

I don't like the guy, but I run toward the screaming. What if he's been caught in a bear trap or something?

As I sprint to where the screaming came from, the shadow moves through the trees. When I round the corner where I think Daren went with his ax, he plows right over me, knocking me into a snowdrift.

"Hey!" I shout.

All I hear is his rapid retreat through the snow and his words, "I'm getting the fuck out of here. Never drinking again!"

Struggling to stand, I slip and fall back into the snow. Panic rises in my throat. Something or someone is here.

That something reaches out a hand to help me stand.

Gulping, I stare first at the hand. Long, bare fingers extend toward me. This person's lack of snow gear would be remarkable if another feature wasn't overpowering everything else. His skin. It glows.

He is the tallest man I've ever seen. But he can't be a man. No man has glowing skin, a braid down to his waist, and—oh no, this isn't natural—pointy ears. The creature's almond-shaped eyes have no irises; they are two vast pools of blackness. His long smooth nose and severe mouth look carved from stone. He is naked except for a strange leather kilt and belt situation. Hands so big that one of them could rip a modestly sized Fraser fir up by the roots.

And the outline in that leather kilt?

Holy clanging silver bells.

Chapter Four

Eldrin

I have her. She's mine now.

"Clara," is all I can muster to say because I'm so overwhelmed by seeing her again.

She and I had never made eye contact before, and something is blocking my throat, making speech difficult.

Her lovely hazel eyes widen in fright when she hears me speak her name. Of course, she's surprised. I'm nothing but a stranger to her, and a terrifying one at that.

"I...did Reba send you? As...a joke?"

A joke?

An odd look comes over her face, and she collapses in peals of laughter.

I have experienced being laughed at before in the elven community. A lot.

Clara laughs too, but it feels different. There is a nuance to it. I know from her sweet aura she is not laughing at me with a mean spirit. She is reacting out of surprise.

We are creatures who take everything so seriously and with a sense of superiority.

My falling in love with a human was the butt of a joke among the other elves. Although my exile would not have been my choice, I was relieved that I never had to hear another creature's chortling at my expense.

Clara's laugh is something else entirely. I never want to escape it. Her laugh starts soft and low, then rises like a tinkling bell. The notes rise higher the more amused she is. When she is so caught up in her laughter that she goes silent is what worries me. At first, I think it's some kind of asphyxiation.

"Do not panic. I will help you, my queen." With both hands, I hold her head still and slant my mouth against hers.

My lips must be some kind of magic because the contact results in her instantly gasping for breath. Clara inhales the breath from my lungs, so much so that I grow dizzy.

Her body struggles against me in her mirth, so I hold her still, moving my hands down to her stomach. Clara jerks and squirms against me, but I press my mouth deeper and notice how my body responds to this new touch.

I've saved her life now, but I don't want to stop this contact. I follow my body's signals and continue. We are kissing now. From what I've observed, this is what humans do as a precursor to mating. I can see why. Kissing my queen is the most thrilling moment of my life.

Clara gasps and writhes as if she's enjoying a game of tickles. This back and forth, with pushing and pulling and tugging and twisting, stirs the parts of my body hidden under my kilt.

The way of humans is becoming more apparent the longer this goes. Every time she pushes against me, the friction causes my cock to expand and increases my desire for her.

The wish to taste more of her overwhelms my senses, and I dart my tongue into her wet mouth. Clara lets out a whimper, and her body softens its rigidity. Something has shifted, and she presses her tongue back against my tongue. Her lips play with my lips. There are interesting, wet noises too. I understand why they call it smooching, because that is the noise our mouths make, and it's delightfully exciting.

As if compelled by some outside force, Clara pulls away from me, covering her mouth. To my shock, she turns and runs.

"Did you not enjoy that, my queen?"

"Nice try, but you're more of a Buddy than a Legolas, pal!"

As I can never be angry at my Clara for this insult, I throw my head back in laughter so loud it shakes the branches up and down the miles of the forest.

Unfortunately, I don't need to run after her, because my tree-shaking laugh has caught her so by surprise that she stops running. Her knees give way, and she falls with a soft thump into a snowbank. My sweet girl has fainted.

Pity.

My feet quickly crunch through the snow to where she lies unconscious. Now, what do I do with a passed-out human? Take her home with me, as planned. This changes nothing.

I suppose I have to get her warm. These creatures are so fragile; it's comical.

Swiftly, I grasp her cold little body against my warm one and scan the woods for the other human.

The male one with the ax quite literally voided his bladder when he saw me, and ran. What kind of a coward leaves another of his species alone in woods haunted by a ferocious elf?

Not that I am going to hurt her. I could never.

I see no sign of the puny man she called Daren with the chemically addled brain. Just as well for him. For revenge for touching one of my trees, I could easily sic a wood sprite to torment him the rest of his days.

I pick up the weapon and carry it with us for the trip home. I have no use for it, but I should make sure it's not here if he comes looking for it again. Or if he, more likely, reports an attack, and someone comes here to investigate.

With my Clara in my arms, my worried brain settles. My heartbeat slows, even more so than what is typical for an elf.

I finally feel calm and at peace, and I know what I have to do with my life now.

Firstly, and always, take care of her.

Inside my hovel, just on the other side of the brook, an eternal fire glows in the fireplace.

Clara is very cold, so I remove the outer layer of her clothing. Setting her down on the hearth rug, I strip off her coat and denim, which have gotten wet in the snow. I toss them into the fire. She'll never need the coat again as she's not ever leaving. And no queen of mine will wear such lowbrow, manmade clothes ever again. An Elf Queen wears only elven cloth.

Her stretchy long underwear is dry, but her woolen hat, scarf, and mittens are soaked through with snow and sweat. I toss them into the fire also.

Even in her sweater and strange underthings, my eyes can see her body is delectable. She will look unearthly beautiful once she's primed and ready for me.

I will not wake her, though. Her tiny human brain is processing what she's just seen, and she needs to sleep. I will sit here with her, acting as her cushion, keeping her warm and comfortable. I'll feed her some of my homemade bread and cheese when she wakes up. Then I'll make some tea and see if there's anything else she requires before the sexual bonding ritual.

My loins stir beneath my leathers at the thought of

engaging in more delightful inter-species pleasures with my Clara.

Most of my fellow elves view these desires as beneath our kind. As a rule, we do not engage in sexual gratification except for procreation alone. Specifically for North Pole elves, we are matched with a partner when we reach the age when reproduction is viable. We have many children, often before the age of 30, and then our libido goes away.

Our reproduction is a very efficient system, but there's no pleasure in it.

And why would there be? We were born to work and serve Nicholas and do his bidding.

As for me, I've been in free fall since my exile was decided. But now, I'm simply free.

I can't wait to get started. I can't wait to fill these woods with a hundred little half-elves with Clara's strength and beauty, and my long life and magic.

Chapter Five

Clara

"Say it with me: I am worthy of love and affection."

I raise my filled wine glass in my right hand and repeat, "I'm worthy of love." I raise my left hand, which holds a tin of peppermint chocolate toffee bark. "And affection!"

Reba shakes her head. "Wine and candy are nice, but they won't love you back."

"Sure they do. They cover me with extra padding to keep me warm in winter."

"Clara. Don't talk about my best friend that way."

"The last guy I met online took me to a pyramid scheme party, and somehow I ended up buying him a seventy-five-dollar kitchen sponge, then he asked me to use it to wash his dishes."

"You just haven't met the right one. I smell Christmas magic in the air."

This conversation replays in my dream as I slowly wake up in my extra-warm bed.

Wait until I tell Reba about the first part of my dream.

The part where a dark-haired, half-naked Legolas finds me in the woods, and he has the outline of the biggest Christmas package I've ever seen. Reba's going to roll her eyes so hard.

I still can't believe Daren freaked out and pushed me out of the way.

"That's it," I say, snuggling deeper into my La-Z-Boy reclining chair, pulling my blanket close around me. "I'm never dating again."

To my alarm, my La-Z-Boy responds in a deep, masculine voice with the diction of a very stern English professor. "That's already out of the question, but I'm happy to hear you say it."

Every inner alarm bell rings, and I bolt upright, eyes flying open.

That's when the facts hit me, and I realize I'm sitting not at home in front of my space heater but in the lap of the creature that came to me in my dream.

"What the actual..."

I scramble away from the huge arms that surround me, or try to, anyway. In my haste, I tumble to the floor.

"Clara," he says. "Have you hurt yourself?"

Cursing, I sort of crab walk away in a truly embarrassing fashion because I do not want to put myself in danger by turning my back on this man...or thing...or whatever he might be.

"Who...what...where..."

And then, the hyperventilating begins.

In my tunnel vision, the elf-ish person stands. I look up, wondering what he's going to do to me, and for half a second, I can see under the leather skirt thing he wears. Oh. My. God.

Although the untouched parts of me light up like a Christmas tree, I know I have to get out of here for my own safety.

And in the future, I have to stay away from the free cider

at Holly Tree farm, because someone spiked it with a hallucinogen.

Throwing the blanket off of me, I face the creature.

"Come back and sit on my lap, Clara, and let me feed you."

"How do you...where am I?" The words tumble out of me in shock and outrage, and fear.

Without an ounce of effort, it seems, the creature picks me up. Up close, his deep, iris-less eyes take me in and mesmerize me. I see flecks of light in their depths like I'm looking at the Milky Way galaxy. For a brief moment, I'm lost in them before I remember myself.

"P-please don't hurt me," I whimper, getting control of my breath and now beginning to tremble.

"You are in shock, I think," he says. "I am sorry for dropping you; I wasn't prepared for you to try to get away from me."

I swallow. "You weren't prepared...you...I...." The trembling turns to a full-on earthquake from within.

"Poor Clara," he croons, but kindly. Not mocking at all.

Once again, we are perched on the floor, and I am wrapped up in a fur blanket and held against his glowing, warm skin.

"Of course, you're shocked. Here is what happened. You and a male of your species wandered into my woods and started chopping down trees. I came out of my home to investigate the intrusion, and scared the puny male specimen away. And to my delight, you remained behind. My Clara. But of course, you must be wondering how I knew your name. That will come later. For now, suffice it to say that we, the elves, know each and every one of you quite intimately. I've been in charge of you for many years."

So not only am I being held against my will by some sort

of supernatural creature, but he thinks he's the boss of me? That's adorable.

"You are out of your tree, m-mister."

"You may call me Eldrin, my queen. My formal name is Eldrin Brynfire the fourteenth, but you may call me El, if you prefer. A queen of a Christmas elf may call her king anything she likes. And I am not out of my tree. We are, more or less, inside of a tree, for lack of a better human explanation."

Okay, this guy is either a next-level cosplayer that Reba hired to play a joke on me. Or...

When I manage to tear my gaze away from his eyes, I take in the bone structure so perfect I want to weep.

I have a strange urge to reach up and trace my fingers over his full, unsmiling lips, high cheekbones, sharp jawline.

Looking down at his body, one thing that makes me smirk is his feet. They are huge, like a human male's feet, but hairless. Gazing at him induces a sense of calm that I don't quite understand.

Smiling, I comment, "You say you're a Christmas elf, but you aren't wearing any striped leggings. Where are the cute little curvy shoes with bells on the toes? And where's your pointy hat?"

Eldrin's eyes go cloudy like a storm in the distance. "Human Christmas movies have characterized us as wee little worker bees dressed in red and green. That is not the case. Humans have mixed up gnomes and elves for centuries. It's embarrassing for you."

He's so sure of himself that it should piss me off. He would piss me off if I weren't so unspeakably aroused. And so, I laugh.

My damn obsession with fantasy books and movies has conjured this person, somehow. My mom and dad always said my interests were concerning. And now I know they were right—my body is ready to dry hump the first magical creature who steps out of the trees. I've never felt such an automatic physical attraction to anyone. Not anyone human, anyway. Legolas was my first crush, human, fantasy and celebrity crush all at the same time.

I'm a mess, and now I'm caught up in some kind of mental breakdown of my own doing.

"You seem out of sorts, still. Is this still a precursor to the bonding ritual, or have we veered off course?"

"Excuse me? Did you say 'bonding ritual'?"

He nods and says matter-of-factly, "The one involving the genitals."

"Oh hell no, Christmas elf."

I squirm in Eldrin's lap to try to move, and the friction of my ass against the Yule log in his kilt alerts me to some actual facts. This man, or whatever, is as rigid as a tree trunk. And huge.

"I'm sorry you're hesitant. It must be obvious that I'm not experienced with sexual bonding. But I assure you, I've studied all the proper instruction manuals, and I think you'll find me adequate."

My brain screams, *Run, you fool!*

My other bits already know just how adequate he is.

Physically, this Eldrin person embodies every sexual fantasy I've ever had. And yet, my body fights with my brain, which remains in fight-or-flight mode. I continue to struggle in his arms, scanning the room for any sign of a doorway to the outside. And yet, I don't hate how much more aroused he seems the more I wiggle and squirm.

What is wrong with me? Did I get hit in the head with a tree branch? Did a Christmas tree fall on me?

"I think I see the problem. I must feed you now. Please sit at the table."

With that, Eldrin stands and sets me down gently on a strange chair made of woody vines that appears to have grown straight up out of the earthen floor. Eldrin's home looks like a circle of trees joined together by walls made of polished precious stones. The ceiling is a mass of tree limbs, dried flowers, herbs, and kitchen tools hanging from them. Along one wall are jars of things that appear to be tinctures, syrups, and infusions of leaves, berries, and fungi.

Before me, Eldrin sets a plate made of wood filled with cheeses, meats, breads, and spreads. "What the hell is this? A charcuterie?"

He hands me a crystal cup filled with wine and smirks. "Where do you think humans came up with the idea?"

I watch him turn to stoke the fire, where he fills a teapot that sits above the flames on some type of cooking surface.

I can't deny that I'm hungry.

"How do I know I can safely eat this?"

Turning back to me, Eldrin picks up the crystal cup and holds it under my nose. The wine has an aroma of sugar plums and hibiscus, and I find that I'm very thirsty for it. He leans down and speaks in a way that I can't tell if he's serious or joking. "What good would it do for me to poison my queen?" He has a point. Or maybe his words have power over me, and his tones slide into my ears and drip down into my nethers. Dampness blooms in my panties.

I take the cup and sip. The warm, spicy wine slides down my throat and quenches my thirst instantly. Forget about free hot cider; he should seriously consider bottling this stuff and selling it. This wine is pure Christmas.

"Hardly beneficial to harm you. It would get in the way of making our half-elf babies together, my queen."

At this, I do a truly ghastly spit take.

Eldrin rests a hand on my back as I dab my face dry. "Are you alright, my queen?"

"Babies?" I croak when I'm barely finished gasping for breath.

His hand radiates heat through my sweater, and I find that my discomfort from sucking wine down the wrong pipe has abated.

I turn to him in amazement. "How did you do that?"

Eldrin's top lip quirks. "Now, do you believe I'm real?"

I don't respond, only bite my lip.

His huge eyes somehow darken even more, and I see my reflection in them. I see how I look to him. A low growl escapes his throat.

"Eat first, then we'll talk. Will that satisfy the precursor requirements to intercourse?"

I snort. "The way you talk is something else."

"I think you'll find I'm well versed in your English vocabulary."

I repeat back at him, imitating his haughty style of speaking. "I think you'll find I'm well versed in your English vocabulary." I crack myself up and have a case of the giggles.

Eldrin is not amused. "I suggest you eat something."

Am I crazy, or does he seem hurt by me? I take a beat to examine his stony expression. Yes, I see now that I shouldn't have mocked him. I know how that feels, all too well.

Perhaps I need to accept his hospitality and then get my wits about me to exit this fever dream without too much trauma.

I tuck into the food he's laid out before me, all too aware that he's crouched right next to me. He watches me intently as I eat. It's unnerving, but the taste of the food makes me forget my self-consciousness. The bread looks like pumpernickel but is softer and more flavorful. The cheese is pungent and tastes so good, along with a smear of something that looks like a mash of herby vegetables. I feel half full after the first bite. The tartness of the cheese is overwhelming, like aged gouda but better. It's so strong that I don't think I would ever eat this if a human tried to feed it to me. But I wouldn't want to insult my captor any more than I already have.

I take a small bite of the chopped stuff, and it tastes nutty, sweet, and salty like the best chutney ever made. And somehow, that's it. Three bites and I'm full. Earlier today—if it's still today, who knows—I had saved up room for tasty holiday treats at the farm, and now I'm stuffed.

"It's all so good," I tell him.

"Elven food has been perfected to keep us nourished in the most efficient amount of time so we can eat quickly and get on with our duties."

I look up into his eyes, suddenly wishing I could see some more feelings in there. But the black orbs only show my reflection. I feel a little sad that that is his existence, but I don't want to say precisely that.

Glancing around the place, I say, "Well, should I leave then? Let you get back to work, doing whatever it is that you do?"

That is my oh-so-subtle way of trying to escape by my wits. The elven food has warmed me thoroughly and given me my strength back. I think I could make it back to my car at Holly Tree Farm from here on foot, even if it's past dark now.

Assuming Eldrin will let me leave. Indeed, he won't keep me here against my will.

Will he? Will I have to break out my taekwondo moves? Would that even work on a magical, mythological creature?

"No. I don't do work for Nicholas anymore."

Nicholas...does that mean Santa Claus? No. That can't be it.

"Alright. You're going to have to explain that."

His brow furrows in confusion. "Truly, this can't be interesting information to you?"

I laugh. "This might all be a dream that could turn nightmarish at any moment, but I assure you none of it is boring. Tell me about this Nicholas."

He sighs and stands up. "Alright, I'll tell you everything."

I'd thought he was about to pace around the room like some kind of orator, but no, he stands because he feels the need to pick me up again. And once again, we are seated in front of the fire, and I am caged in his arms like a pet. I've stopped scanning the room to look for an exit. And now, I'm not sure I have any hope of leaving.

Maybe, just maybe, I do not want to leave. Yet.

Eldrin begins his story. "Every Christmas elf has a contingent of human children to look after, record their behavior, and report back to Nicholas."

My jaw drops. I have no words.

"Well," he continues. "How else do you think Old White Beard manages a Naughty or Nice list? Think he does all that organizing himself? He loves to take all the credit.

"Along with thousands of other children all over the world, you were one of my charges. Unbeknownst to you, of course. Humans are not supposed to be aware that we're surveilling their every move.

"When you think about it, it's a pretty terrible system. Determining whether or not a child deserves a gift based on whether they made too many bad decisions at a time when their brains haven't fully developed yet. Who does that? The current man in charge is the answer to that.

"We Uncommon elves, possessing a life span of six to seven hundred years, have the magical ability to teleport, remain invisible, and to be in more than one place at a time. So the List Making fell to us. The Common elves' magic is limited to crafting, building, and manipulating nature, making them the perfect candidates for Santa's workshop.

"Yet the big elf in the red suit likes to let everyone assume he does all of it—making the toys and maintaining the lists.

"But it wasn't always that way. Previous Nicholases were far less interested in glory. It wasn't until this one took over in the middle of your nineteenth century that gift-giving was based on human merit.

"I'm still one of the younger elves, but I know my history. Maybe my rebellious young ways landed me in my current predicament.

"It goes against our code to form attachments to humans. It goes against our code to fall in love at all. And to fall in love with a human is something the elven community likes to sweep under the rug...until it starts to 'cause problems.'

"Those so-called problems began almost the second you, Clara, were placed in my charge. I wanted nothing more than to make myself visible and be your friend. You were such a lonely girl who only asked for books for Christmas, and I made sure you received all the books you asked for and more."

A strange sensation sweeps through my stomach. "I did. I always had books," I murmur. Eldrin smiles. I'm starting to fall for this charade, or whatever this is.

"Of course, I doctored your lists to include fantasy, science fiction, anything at all that I knew would possibly connect you to my world. It was futile, I knew that. And even the best human stories of elves and elven lore are woefully watered down. Still, I was desperate for any kind of connection with you."

Although I am still processing all of this, Eldrin skips on to another subject—the only subject he seems interested in. "You have eaten. When do we commence with the mating?"

Studying his eyelids and his facial expressions, I'm beginning to be able to tell where he's looking and what he's staring at.

And right now, it's the same thing almost all men stare at. "If I say no, will it matter?"

Eldrin sits up straight as if offended. "Of course it matters.

I don't want to touch someone who does not wish to be touched. The thought of that is vile to me."

I nod, sure that my relief is visible. "Would you let me leave if I asked to leave?"

He smiles in that amused way he did before. "That I cannot do."

"Why not?"

"Because you are the entire reason for my exile, and you are my only key to happiness."

"But if you love me like you think you do, you should set me free."

Eldrin laughs. "Then you will run and tell all the other humans about me, and you may never come back. That scenario is unacceptable. I will just have to work harder to make you fall in love with me."

His black eyes change. Somehow, they grow darker, more intense. The stars in them have gone out, and now he takes on the look that is less elfish and dignified, and more wolfish. He's another species, I remind myself. A wild thing. Be careful.

His primal, singularly focused expression sends a shiver down my back, and I can't decide if it's a fearful shiver or an aroused kind.

"Fall in love with you? You are a trip."

Eldrin cups my face in his two large, glowing hands and angles his face toward me without another word.

The excellent food has given me enough mental fortitude that I could pull myself away and send him flying with a roundhouse kick to his sugar plums and candy cane. Maybe.

Except that I'm not sure I want to. My mind and body have stopped fighting each other, and I am starting to accept that I contain worlds of contradictions. I'll forgive myself tomorrow. Will I be forgiving myself for losing my virginity to a cosplayer? Is there a worse-case scenario? It's all very fuzzy, and the cosplayer scenario now seems to be the most unlikely.

Also, a hallucination is not likely. I now remember everything that happened to the point of passing out, and I know I hadn't consumed anything other than water this morning before the trip to the farm. I neither drank from Daren's flask nor consumed mushrooms in these woods.

So what does this mean? Those ears don't look like prosthetics. There's no device or phenomenon that I know of that could make a human's skin glow like that. Plus, the healing hands, how he knew about my books, and my lonely childhood.

It doesn't seem like it could be true, but there's no other explanation. I'm in the arms of a bona fide Christmas elf.

Eldrin's smooth, angular lips are so close to mine I can feel his breath against them. He says, "This is how I've seen human beings kiss. Tell me, is the kissing more enticing now that you've been fed and entertained?"

My lashes flutter. Here's my chance. If I say no, his principles might let me leave. But instead, I say, "Only if you stop talking like an alien."

Logic, reason, and self-preservation have flown out the window.

"I am happy to talk to you however you wish," he says, his voice now sounding less prideful and condescending and more...hungry.

I like it.

I reach up and touch his face. I swallow hard and debate with myself. Demand him to let me leave or give in to what he wants...and to what my body wants.

I always said I wanted to lose my virginity to Legolas.

Whether or not this is real, I'm going to make the most of it.

Chapter Six

ELDRIN

"There's something you need to know first," my queen says to me. "I'm a virgin, and I've seen what's under that kilt. It's going to take a lot of foreplay to—ah—do the bonding ritual, as you say."

"Foreplay," I say the word out loud, recalling my limited knowledge of that aspect. I hadn't read enough about that.

"What does that require?"

She smiles up at me flirtatiously, fluttering her lashes in a very pleasing way. "Well. It depends on the person. For me, I really like for someone to make me feel safe."

I nod. "Very well. What or who shall I kill for you?"

She snorts, and it's a strange sound that squeezes my heart.

"No, Eldrin. We start with you holding me."

From what I had read at one time. I thought kissing was a precursor for the sex ritual, but this human seems different. She seems to require that I hold her first, much like I did after she had fainted.

"Oh, I…" I trail off as Clara makes herself comfortable against me, leaning her cheek against my chest. The sitting and holding seem unnecessary, as I'm already quite aroused, and my shaft is indeed pressing into her leg. And I can smell her pheromones. She's quite ready.

But If she is content for me to wrap her up against me like this, I am happy. Whatever my queen wants, my queen gets.

"What is this called?"

"This? This is hugging and cuddling," she says, her voice muffled against my bare chest. "It relaxes me, and it builds trust. Trust is a big part of sex, especially for a twenty-something virgin like me who's been saving herself for the right moment."

I don't mind it, but I don't understand this strange feeling that builds inside my body cavity, somewhere near my sternum.

"Am I doing it right, my queen?"

Clara's sweet face nuzzles against my skin, and she laughs softly. It is thrilling just to feel her breathing, to know she's here with me. "Well, you're even better than my La-Z-Boy at home, so you'll do."

I do not like this. "What is a Lazy Boy? Do you have someone in your house who does nothing but allows you to sit on his lap like this? Show him to me so I can send him away. He will be crying for his mother before I am through with him."

Again, Clara makes the noise of a piglet that makes me smile. Her laughing noises warm my loins even though my anger grows the more I picture Clara sitting on someone other than myself.

"Oh, you sweet man. Elf. Whatever. It's the name of a chair. A very nice, squishy chair. It's not a man."

This makes me feel better.

"I'm sorry, I don't have a lot of proper human furniture, but I can service you any way you like."

At this, she leans back away from my chest, and I do not like that feeling. Clara looks up into my eyes and squints. "I wish Reba were here because you, sir, are something else."

"I would like you to rest your head on my chest again. I want to see something," I say.

Giggling, she obeys, but this time she wraps her arms around my torso and squeezes. There is a rush of warmth through my body. I am familiar with the concept of chemicals and hormones in humans. Still, the elven anatomy doesn't work the same, or at least I hadn't thought so.

"Why does this cuddling thing you like also make me feel things?"

She sighs, and this time her breath causes tiny bumps to appear on my skin. "That is oxytocin."

I correct her. "Elves don't produce that."

"If cuddling feels good, then you most definitely do. Have you never been cuddled before? Not even as a baby?"

"I was carried at my mother's breast until I was able to walk and talk at the age of three months. That is normal for us."

My queen is silent for a moment. I can sense something is wrong. But instead of pulling away, she squeezes me tighter, to the point where I feel there will be an imprint of her on my torso. I would love that if it were possible.

I feel good protecting her; that much is true. I know that this rush of chemicals through my body is also equal in strength to sexual arousal. This makes the end goal confusing, but perhaps human goals are different? Maybe she and I are different from other creatures with overpowering instincts to mate. Except, no. I need to breed her as soon as possible.

Before I met Clara, I had thought protection amounted to

clothing her, warming her, sheltering her, and killing predators with my arrows in the forest.

This is different, and I don't comprehend it. But I like it. Maybe this is what it feels like when elves fall for humans? I wish I knew someone to ask. I know that half-elves, half-humans exist somewhere. But they, too, are exiled.

This strange desire to protect more than her physical being...it must fall into the realm of human emotions. Emotional safety is something I don't quite understand as an elf. Still, I'm beginning to feel the other side of that. I feel happy knowing that I'm needed for something like this. It costs me nothing and keeps her still. She isn't trying to run away while my arms are around her. I can smell the chemical reaction in her pheromones. Soon, she will be ready for me, both in body and spirit. But I've learned since meeting her that I should not say things so...clinically.

"Can you help me better understand what else you need?" I ask Clara.

Her face peers up at me. I look down at her huge hazel eyes and lose myself in the flecks of gold and green. Her skin doesn't glow in the same way that mine does, but her luminescence of spirit gives her face a softness that entrances me.

My eyes watch her thoroughly, glossy lips as she explains. "Just be you, and tell me why you chose me."

Her smile pierces my heart. "I have watched you from a distance for so long, but I could always feel the bigness of your heart. I watched you smile at others but never at me. I longed for that. And now, nothing compares to seeing you up close. You are warm and soft, and I feel connected to you. Even now, I can feel your human blood pumping harder in your veins. Does that also happen when you hug people, normally?"

Clara blinks up at me. "Oh. No, not especially. Usually, hugging helps to sort of settle the blood pressure."

"I am very sorry. Then I must be doing this wrong because

yours is not settled at all. In medical terms, you may be close to danger."

Shaking her head and biting her lip, I sense that she is shy in responding to this news about her blood pressure. "It's a normal reaction to...arousal."

"Then I am delighted. Shall we begin kissing?"

Her eyes grow wide, and once again, I think I have said the wrong thing.

But no, that's not what has happened. She rests her small hands on my chest and looks into my eyes with a plea in her expression. Her tongue darts out to moisten her lips, and the sight of that pink tongue makes my wand inside my kilt strain to make contact with it.

Gently I press my lips to Clara's.

Her kiss is so much better now that she's not resisting. I've stared at her glossy lips all day and craved their softness. Her full lips fit against mine, and they are sweet like candy. She feels and tastes like plump fruit. I'm suddenly aware that the kissing is not just to service a woman's readiness, but it also spikes my need for her. I have been reading the wrong books. Everything leading up to the mating is just as enjoyable for me as it is for her. The feeding, the talking, the laughing, the snuggling, and the kissing. I love all of it. I love all of Clara.

The dance of our lips heightens my awareness of her hands which palm my chest and run over my shoulders and down my arms, making me feel wanted and savored.

Her eyes open when she feels the nudge of my straining cock.

Her cheeks flush. Her nostrils flare.

I want to be closer, and I need to make her wetter.

I shift my queen, so her luscious thighs straddle my hips; she gasps in surprise at my effortless movements.

"You will have to get used to my easy manipulations." I don't want to brag out loud, as I'm beginning to understand humans don't like that. But it's true. In addition to being bigger and stronger, we elves are supernaturally graceful. I could just as quickly bend her over and take her from behind without breaking a sweat.

For now, I'm happy to have my queen wrapped around me and her lips exploring my lips. This way, I can feel and smell her heat and her dampness. I don't know how she would react if she knew that, so I keep it to myself.

I run my hands over her backside and squeeze. Clara gasps, then fixes her arms around my neck, dragging her warm pussy over my bulge.

"Oh gods," I rasp at this teasing friction.

Cramming my hands down the waistband of her long underwear, I slide over her juicy rump and reach down her split, the fingers of both hands landing between her folds.

Clara gasps and jerks her lips away from mine, eyes wide in surprise. "El," she whispers.

I begin to move my fingers through her wetness, pulling her folds apart. My mouth nips her neck. "Yes, my queen."

It pleases me to feel her essence drip down my fingers when I call her "my queen."

The whimpering from her drives me dangerously close to climax. I kiss her again, and I feel her tongue swipe against my lip. It's a curious, erotic sensation.

I am overcome by all the things she's doing to my body. I had not been prepared to feel this good. "My love. Now is the time to tell you I have fantasized about this moment, but I am overwhelmed by how sweet this is. I have spent myself in my bed thinking about you, missing you. My imaginings are very powerful, but I had no idea. But I have to tell you...."

As I ramble on, Clara's sweetness soaks my hands. Her lips brush lightly against mine, and the feeling is so sweet that it triggers that feeling of attachment she explained to me before. I only sensed jealousy, lust, and obsession before she was in my arms; now, I don't know if I can ever stop touching her. I never want to leave her side.

She wiggles, nestling in closer, rubbing the front of her pussy against my cock. My gods, the throbbing ache to be inside her is overwhelming. I am dangerously close to climaxing.

My sweet Clara whispers, "You look like you need to tell me something, El. Don't be shy. Remember, it's my first time, too."

This feeling of trust has triggered so many emotions, I don't know how to sort through them. I believe she speaks the truth. "My seed is going to be wasted before I've pleased you," I tell her.

Slowly, a look of understanding comes across her face.

"Oh, El. That's okay," she breathes, again killing me with her radiant smile. "We've got so much time to make the half-elf babies."

My whole being is flooded with relief and joy. I am not used to this attitude; our culture places so much value on efficiency that any wasted spend is frowned upon. "How do I love you more than I did one minute ago, Clara?"

Her big, hazel eyes go hooded, and she leans back away from me, pulling her sweater off over her head.

For the first time, I am presented with breasts, and they are a work of art. Clara's are cradled in a swath of red lace with a holly leaf decoration.

"Festive," I remark, unable to take my eyes away from them. My hands come back around to her front, and I caress her round curves, which yield under my touch. "Do you know how to take this off? There's a latch in the front."

I examine the simple closure and answer her literally. "Yes."

She huffs out a small laugh. "Well, take it off then."

Curious, I ask, "Is this a part of the foreplay, other than managing the clitoris?"

Again, her smile. It radiates through me. "You know, I'm starting to warm up to the way you talk. And yes. If you want me to be ready to take you, teasing my nipples will help." As she says the words, she blushes in her innocence. I feel honored that she speaks so plainly with me without mocking my inexperience.

I swiftly remove the lacey thing that grips her round breasts together. Her breasts spill out before me, flushed, with nipples taut and tempting as two spicy ginger snaps. My cock aches to spill its load inside my queen, and I keep having to remind myself that there are no rules here.

My Clara may not love me, but she is as good as my wife once we mate.

I give in to the strange urge to touch and taste each nipple, memorizing the way these abundant curves feel against my palms. My people use these for nurturing babies only. But the pleasure this gives me, and the pleasurable moans she responds with, sends fire raging through my veins.

Needing to know more, I cup her mound again, noticing she's absolutely soaked. An involuntary growl resonates in my chest. I want to be on top of her, to maul her with my mouth, to impale her on my cock. This woman is driving me mad with need.

"Clara," I rumble, barely recognizing my own voice.

She nods. "Lay me down. It's time."

It takes no time at all to move us to the bed, where I watch my queen remove the rest of her strange underthings. My kilt tossed aside, I follow Clara's gaze.

"Will you spread for me now, my lovely one?"

I hope she is not only going along with all of this just to appease me. There have been stories of elves who do not enjoy the fragment of a libido they are given. I would not want that for my queen. But when she spreads her legs for me, any doubt about her arousal dissipates.

"I'm ready," she says, pulling me down on top of her.

Towering over her, I let my cock find its way home between her folds. I coat myself in her sweetness and allow her to guide the tip inside her cunt.

Just the tip is almost too big for her, and I stop, even as her muscles grip me.

"El, I know what you're thinking. I can take it."

"I must stretch you slowly."

Again, I'm delighted at the sharing of more warm kisses with our tongues. Clara's back arches off the bed, pushing me to drive deeper. I stretch her slowly, bit by bit, savoring every whisper, every moan, every whine. She bites down on her bottom lip as her eyes flutter close. I lean in and press my face against hers, feeling her warmth against my cheek. I stretch more. Her hot muscles clench, relax, and finally take all of me to the hilt. I groan in the pleasure and the pain of it; she's almost too tight. I have no business fucking a human, but I cannot stop. Not when she wants me, needs me.

Her body relaxes and fits against me, and my heart is so happy that everything lets go. I spill my seed inside her, without the pleasure I know is required of me to give her.

"Gods. Clara!"

My cum fills her, and I clamor to find her sweet spot so she can have her release.

Through the awe and lovely stupor following my climax, my thumb searches for her clit. The way her face changes when I find it, and the motion of her writhing body under me, causes my cock to harden all over again.

I continue to nudge her along with my thumb and kiss her warm mouth until I feel a violent tremble take hold.

"El!" Her release rolls over her, and she grips me close,

clasping her arms around me and pulling the full weight of me down on top of her.

We hold each other still like this for several breathless moments, only gazing into each other's eyes. My hardness returns and my body takes over. I begin to thrust.

Clara smiles and arches into me, demanding more.

"I can't believe you're already hard again," she murmurs.

The smirk is uncontrollable. "Told you, our species is highly efficient."

Clara licks one swollen lip and says, "Oh, tell me more about the efficiency of your workshop, daddy."

I'm trying to parse this request while my body acts on its own, thrusting in and out steadily.

"Well...well...you see... I'm sorry, what was the question, my queen?"

Her sweet laughter is accompanied by a firm grip of her sex, and my body rejoices.

<h1 style="text-align:center">Chapter Seven</h1>

So this is not a sex dream. Legolas never took the time to stretch me, nor did he pump me so hard in the end.

Good lord.

We sit together on the rug, wrapped in the most luxurious blankets that have ever touched my skin. My head rests in Eldrin's lap as I gaze into the crackling fire.

His fingers play with my hair, and I might drift off to sleep any minute.

"I am confused about one thing, my queen."

"Mm?"

"I didn't see any blood."

It takes a second to realize what he's saying, and then I know.

"Oh. That. Being a virgin doesn't necessarily mean that the hymen isn't broken. A lot of time, they break on their own. Sports, biking, groin injuries. And, well, toys."

"Which toys?" Eldrin asks, confused. "I know many things about toys, despite not having been a toymaker in Nicholas's workshop."

I lift one eyebrow and turn my head to look up at him. "I'll bet you do. I'm talking about toys for sex. Sex toys. You know, vibrators, dildos, the list goes on and on."

Eldrin appears to be at a loss for words for the first time. "They make toys for that? Who makes those? Santa does not have those at his workshop, I can assure you."

I laugh so hard at this I might throw up.

"What has happened? Are you ill?"

I continue wheeze-laughing, which turns into silently shaking and holding my stomach, which turns into crying.

"But what if I...." I shriek between gales of laughter, "What if I put it on my Christmas list... Hey Santa, I've been very good. Can I please have a clit sucker..."

I have lost control of my bodily functions, and Eldrin's confusion just makes me laugh harder.

"I do not have any medicine for human hysterics, but I can offer you some tea."

"Oh my god. I love you," I say, wiping my eyes.

His face lights up. "Then this has been a successful meeting of the minds. I'm pleased that you love me in return."

He sucks in a trembling breath.

"El?"

The back of his hand dabs his cheek. "Why are my eyes leaking?"

I sit up and look at him in alarm and see what is happening.

"' Good gods, why are humans so fragile?'" I say, in an imitation of him. "'Now, why are my eyes leaking?' My dear sweet Eldrin. You have feelings. Do elves not cry?"

He swipes again at his face, and I melt as I see his chin tremble. "We cry over stories of great bravery and sacrifice. We cry when we grieve a loss. But I don't understand this... I'm happy. I've never been this happy in my entire life, and yet I'm crying."

Once again. I crawl into his lap. I kiss away the tears, kiss his tender lips, place a kiss on his forehead and wrap him in the tightest hug I can muster. "I call them the happy-sads. When you're so happy, you don't know what to do with yourself but emote. Does that help?"

"It's true...and there is something else. One day, you're going to die. Sooner than what is acceptable to me. And I will be alone."

For this, I have no solution or good answer.

Because it's true, I do love this haughty, strange creature in my arms. And it is equally unacceptable that we won't grow old together on his terms.

I rub my hands over his arms and chest. "All I know how to do is enjoy the moments we have, then. And I'll stay for as long as you want me to stay."

He shakes his head. "You can't leave even if I wanted you to leave. We are married now. We performed the bonding ritual."

I pull back and study his face. "What do you mean, we are married now? You dick me, and we're married? That's not how it works, El."

"I suppose I hadn't made that clear enough. In my culture, we are married now. And it is very likely that we made a child. Or two. I lost count."

"Excuse me?!"

He explains. "Every release from me draws down another egg. May I remind you of our efficiency?"

I do the math in my head. "Are you saying that every time you nut in me, I could get pregnant? What if we did it eight times in a day?"

Eldrin beams at me. "Then I would be the proudest of all elves. No one has produced eight at once."

I stand up, gripping the blanket around my nakedness. I hiss, "I would be the Octomom! I could die!"

My lover stands, alarmed. "Die? No."

My arms flail, and I start to panic. "Did the sex manuals tell you about the mortality rate of women delivering multiples? Because I don't know, but I think I need to look that up!"

Eldrin places his hands on my shoulders. "There is nothing to panic about yet. We only did it twice. We will abstain until after the baby is born. But as you are a human, I don't know if the multiples thing applies here." While he's scratching his head, I pace the room.

I come back to face him. "Tell me, what exactly type of manuals have you been reading?"

"The educational ones."

I nod, breathing slowly and calming myself. "No watching porn?"

He shrugs. "Screens do nothing for me. I suspect it's why we do not create electronics in Santa's workshops. The glow is harsh and offensive to our eyes. But I have access to any human books I want."

I look around the place, which is devoid of books. "How do you get them?"

"This is where you will have to accept another layer of magic, but it may take some time to understand. We can speak to trees and plants, even dead ones. Books are made of wood pulp, and those trees still carry energy that speaks to other trees. I can read virtually anything made of paper just by communing with the trees. What's the matter? You look skeptical, my sweet Clara."

I shake my head. "No erotica?"

"I do not think so."

"Not even romance?"

"What is romance other than what your dictionary says?"

I suck in a long breath. "Oh, honey. You need to go for a walk in the woods."

Chapter Eight

Eldrin

This suggestion to take a walk might be part of a plot to run away.

My little snow bunny must know by now she cannot outrun me. Now that I've had her, there's no other path for me. I'm keeping her.

I think she rather enjoyed herself, too, and I might be able to convince her to let me take her again soon.

Still, that glint in her eye is full of mischief. It's both maddening and arousing. Clara confounds me at every turn.

So, I tell her she must accompany me.

"What do you mean, go with you?" she asks, wide-eyed and pouty. "I promise to stay put if you leave me here. It's too cold out there, especially since you burned my coat in the fire."

She makes me laugh. Her attitude changes when I produce a long, white robe. "That manufactured abomination does not belong in my world. This is what a queen wears. Besides, you do want to see some real magic, don't you?" The long coat glitters in the firelight like fresh snow. I help her slip her arm into it; she gasps softly as the material brushes against her skin.

"I've never felt anything like this. Is it silk?"

"No," I tell her. "It is elven made."

The length of it reaches down to her ankles and wrists like it was measured precisely for her.

I smile as I watch her touch the fur lining the neck and the wrists. "This *is* magic. This feels softer than angora, and the stones and the beadwork ... I've never seen patterns like this before," she marvels.

Clara touches my heart. Seeing my world through her eyes is its own kind of magic. I'm looking at my queen, dressed in a robe fit for royalty. I scarcely feel I have the right to touch her, yet I can't resist touching her soft cheek and pressing a kiss to her forehead. "You look like a proper snow queen," murmur, in awe.

She smiles, spinning around and making the long cloak twirl about her. "Eat your heart out, White Witch."

"Ah. Narnia. Confusing book. Lions would never survive in the snow, and witches, as a rule, do not turn people to stone out of revenge. Some strange Christmas mythology you humans have."

She laughs but doesn't argue. "You think that's strange? Have you seen the Elf on the Shelf?"

The only thing keeping the bile rising in my throat at the mere mention of those vile little dolls is the fact that I'm gazing at my own personal goddess. "Abominations," I growl. Moving this outing along, I produce a long sash of elven material and wrap it around Clara's waist. The other end, I fasten around my hand.

"Am I a dog on a leash?"

I arch one eyebrow. "More like a skittish little snow bunny."

Clara responds by making a big show about the injustice of it all. "Oh my. What a wicked elf you are."

I squint down at her, letting her know that I'm not buying her song and dance. "Humans are indeed strange creatures."

"No, it's just me," she replies. The quick wink she gives nearly compels me to postpone this outing in the woods and bend her over my knee. But this is for the sake of our relationship.

Gripping her hand in mine, we transition to the outside. I keep my eyes on her, thrilled at how shocked she is. We were in my hovel, and now we're outside. No door. Just here, and then there. Where once there was a golden room glittering with fire and stones, and all the coziness and cheer of the holidays, is now an icy blue forest and a gusting wind.

I'd better make this quick.

Chapter Nine

Clara

Oddly, though the wind whips my face, the coat feels as if I'm utterly impervious to cold. This is a magic level of warmth.

Still, my nose hairs are beginning to stick together. "Okay, friend. Touch your tree, and let's go home."

Eldrin turns to me, a triumphant smile on his lips. "Home?"

I square my shoulders. "Well, it's not as if you're going to let me escape, so I meant your home. Wherever is warm is home. Let's get on with it."

I'm confused, but I follow as he touches one tree after another, muttering to himself.

"Are you lost? Don't you have like a Dewey Decimal System of your...tree energy or whatever?"

"You do have so many questions."

"About this brand new magical world you've kidnapped me into? Are you surprised?"

"Good point. I should have factored in how difficult the transition would be for you."

That's an unsettling word. "Transition?"

"You're adaptation from your world to mine. I hadn't thought that part through. I only knew you belonged to me. But I understand your happiness in this new life is essential, so I'll do my best."

Chuckling through my shivering, I say, "Like my grandmother used to say, 'If Mama ain't happen, ain't nobody happy.'"

He blinks at me as his brain parses what I've said. "Your happiness is assured, my Clara. Perhaps later you can explain some of these interesting human sayings."

Eldrin doesn't give me any further reassuring looks or words. He only furrows his brow in concentration as he runs his hands along the bark of tree after tree.

"Ah. I found it. Now stay quiet while I read."

I mutter, "Can you check these books out and take them home? Because my face is freezing."

In response, Eldrin gives a rough tug to the sash connecting us, and my body slams against him. Keeping one hand on the old hardwood tree, he heats my entire face, fingers, toes—everywhere—with the warmth that radiates from his glowing skin. He's like a walking space heater out in the freezing forest, a fact that isn't quite as noticeable inside his cozy home.

Reluctantly allowing myself to mold against him, I whisper, "You'd better find one of those romances with a good grovel in it after telling me I ask too many questions."

Eldrin's face begins to change. A yellow glow shines against his cheek, casting him in a light that's more brilliant than his already-luminous skin. I look for the source of it. I see that the radiance emanates from his hand resting against the tree. It's glowing brighter than the rest of him at the moment.

"My Queen gives good advice. I see what I have done now. I have hurt your feelings. I am sorry."

I open my mouth to ask which book, exactly, he's reading, but he lets go of the sash to press his two fingers over my lips. "Just a moment. Let me finish reading."

I have to stifle a laugh. This is the same face I make at Reba when she interrupts my reading.

A part of me wonders if I will ever see Reba again. It's not sadness I feel, but I do sense the loss. It's strange how neutral I feel about it, which disturbs me.

I feel sad that I don't feel anything more than that.

I cover the elven fingers that press against my lips. I need to be reminded that I can, in fact, feel things. I kiss those fingers as he reads.

Eldrin's black eyes glitter, and his stony lips twitch. The heat from his hand warms my lips. I put the tips of those fingers between my teeth and scrape, watching his eyes hood.

There can't be any human bedroom eyes that look half as sexy as elven bedroom eyes. It feels like seducing a god in the middle of some critical work, and it juices me up.

I gently lick, watching his nostrils flare.

With the slow slide of my tongue up the underside of his middle finger, I show my lover what I would do for him. Taking the cue, Eldrin curls his fingers into my mouth, and I welcome them in. Sucking, teasing the tips with my tongue. The ever-present glow in his face brightens, and his eyes darken. He now appears less human and more monster, and I could not crave him more.

I pop his fingers out of my mouth. "Tell me what you're reading, El."

He opens his lips, baring his teeth. I feel like he's about to give orders. Make me kneel and take it out. And I would. I would spring him free and take all of that in my mouth and let him drain his essence down my throat and choke me with it.

But he doesn't do that. Instead, the intense light in his hands dims back to normal, and his hands cupping my face nearly singes me with its heat.

"Clara. I know what I have to do now. I'm sorry. I'm sorry for criticizing your inquisitiveness. That's not what you are to me."

"And do you apologize for saying I'm fragile? And for neglecting to tell me before the sex happened that in your culture, we'd already be married?"

He nods. "I apologize, and I apologize again. But you are not obliged to forgive. In nature, when we damage something, we have to create balance. When someone dies, someone else is born. When we hurt, we heal. So if you'll let me."

I would never have expected this man, or creature, to kneel in front of me. "Clara. You are none of those things. You are not exhausting. You give me life. You are not a headache; you are a balm. Fragile? No, you are far stronger than any creature on this earth. But one thing I cannot make amends for is claiming you as my queen. That, you still are and always will be. I am sorry for not telling you that the mating ritual means we are wed before you consented to it. I've been very clumsy from the beginning. Cast me aside if you must, but just know that we will be linked for eternity regardless. You may move on, but I will live in misery."

I fight hard to control my smile. "Is this speech something you learned in one of those books?"

"Yes. Is it working?"

"Possibly. What else have you learned?"

"That I should be giving you an entirely different type of tongue lashing."

Oh god. That long tongue. Not gonna lie. I kind of want to see what that does to me.

"Let's proceed, then," I say.

Eldrin, still kneeling, opens my coat, buries his face between my thighs, and inhales deeply.

"The scent of my elven queen."

Did he say, elven queen? He's deluded. I can't just turn into a creature like him.

And at the moment, I don't care because his oversized noggin is nudging my thighs apart. His face nuzzles my sex, making me slick with need.

With a deep growl that vibrates up my spine, Eldrin bares his teeth and takes my long johns between his teeth. As if made of tissue paper, the fabric shreds under the strength of one quick tug.

A blast of icy air chills the newly exposed skin of my lower half, but I immediately forget the cold because my elf king is in control of my body. His hands grip my thighs and swiftly hooks my legs over his shoulders, burying his face in my sex.

I gasp. "Oh. Here? Outside? Oh...okay."

I'm not entirely sure what to do with my hands, as nobody has ever done anything like this to me before. So, I reach up and hold on to a tree branch while Eldrin kisses and teases my split with his lips and tongue.

I feel him everywhere, and not just my groin.

My coat barely covers us from the full view of the woods, and anyone walking by will see what's happening. I figure this is just a bit of play before the real thing, but then his tongue splits me open, and he nestles his face...right...there.

Holy shit.

I bite down so hard I might split my lip. The noise that comes out of my mouth is drowned out by El's primal growls and snarls. I wouldn't have thought such a high-born creature was capable of sounding so beastly.

"Oh my god," I gasp as his tongue dives into my entrance.

He hums his enjoyment, the vibrations doing scandalous things to my body.

I arch my back, and the coat falls open. I look down and see that dark braid. I reach my hand down, take hold of it, and grind my body against his face. I might die if I don't get my release.

But when I open my eyes again, we're no longer in the woods but back in Eldrin's hovel, the crackling flame and the soft glow warming my skin.

I don't think anything about this situation could surprise me anymore.

Until he rises to his feet. Gasping, I grip the braid tighter. My thighs clamp over his ears. Anything I can do to hold steady, I do it.

If I fall off of him, I might break my neck.

But if this is my last moment in life, maybe it's worth it.

Chapter Ten

My Clara's taste is, incredibly, even better than her scent. She has permeated every part of my being. Her essence on my tongue intoxicates me. She is more potent than the most poisonous plant, and I may drown in her nectar.

One tongue is not enough to explore and please all of her in all the ways I want to please her.

There is time. Not enough time, when one compares a human life to that of an elf. But I will not ruin the moment by thinking of that inevitable soul-crushing pain.

I am full of knowledge and understanding now. The kissing, the hugging, the cuddling. Even the talking. It finally makes sense.

Clara's muscles clamp down on my tongue, and the rest of her trembles.

I back my tongue out to find the taut, erect button at the top of her slit.

When I savor her there, Clara's reaction almost sends the

two of us toppling to the floor. She needs to writhe on me, rub against me. I move us to the bed to give her more control and safety, gently lowering her onto her back.

"Take off the coat. Let me see and taste all of you."

I will stop at nothing to make sure I am attached to Clara in every way.

As my mouth lays waste to her core, my Clara comes harder than the last time. This Christmas elf shall wreck the sweet human for anyone else. Further, I intend to ruin her for sex toys. A clit sucker? What's that? Me. I'm the clit sucker.

After I've drawn out another orgasm from my queen, I must have more.

"Clara. I want to try something I read about—"

"Have at it, El," she interrupts, kissing my lips, now coated with her essence.

I lie down on my back and pull Clara over me to sit on my face. She faces my legs, her hands resting on my torso. And I am in heaven.

"Oh, my god," she breathes.

"Massage me while I drink from you," I command.

I tongue kiss her swollen, wet folds, and her nearly-limp body twitches to life again.

"Should I hover? I don't want you to suffocate, El."

She makes me laugh. "To me, you weigh nothing, tiny human. Smother me with your pussy."

Heat races through her veins. I can smell it. The joy of knowing I can speak to her and make her heart pound — it is indescribable.

But it's nothing compared to the vicious devouring of each other that follows: the accompanying obscene noises, her moans, her squirts, her shattering climax. When I think neither of us has anything left to give, there's always more.

That's when my Clara gives me the gift of her sweet mouth on my cock.

Her lips wrap around the tip and take me in, while at the same time, I fuck her with my mouth. It seems like we are one creature, both giving and receiving. I feel my soul elevate from my body as she rides my face.

She uses me like a candy cane, and I can barely stand it. Yet, I don't want her to stop.

"Clara," I exclaim, my voice muffled between her folds.

She keeps going, slowly. Soon, we begin to buck against each other, having built each other up to a level of desperation I didn't think was possible. Finally, I reach down, giving in to the urge to grab hold of Clara's hair.

My free hand lifts her off my face, and I hardly have the breath to speak. "Clara. I don't want to hurt you, but I must...."

Her mouth pops my erection free, and she gives me her approval. "Yes, king. Pull my hair and fuck my mouth."

With a growl, I wrap her hair around my fist and do what I need to do with her.

"My gods. My queen is not a human but a goddess."

Chapter Eleven

I have no idea how long I've been trapped in here with my elf, now my husband, apparently.

My prison has become a love nest, and one I never want to leave.

Now that I've figured out that there are no doors, and we simply flit in and out at Eldrin's command, I couldn't just walk out anyway.

My elf and I have spent long hours trying all manner of wicked delights, carefully avoiding any more "inseminations," as El puts it.

Sleeping next to someone who radiates heat is a dream for someone like me, always cold.

El is so sweet with me, wrapping me up under a pile of blankets, insisting I use his body as a mattress.

"I must feel you on me at all times. When I drift off to sleep, I will panic if I wake up and don't feel you nearby."

The truth is, I find it endearing and wonderful.

"I have been on many dates with men I've met online, hoping I had met the one. This last one with that guy was the worst ever. But then I met you, and it turned out to be the best. Maybe I should send Daren a thank you note," I tease.

El growls. "Your pissant date is not welcome in these woods, or he will be subjected to a far worse punishment."

I giggle. "So sexy when you're surly like that."

My husband rolls me over and caresses my belly. "And you should be punished too for coming to my woods to choose a Christmas tree."

I sit up in bed and stare down at him, ready to defend myself.

"I wasn't planning on stealing any of your trees. I'll have you know I meant to choose a tree from the farm. Totally above board."

I see the evil grin on El's face and know he's teasing me. I wish there were hair on his chest to pull because I would. "You're becoming a little too human with your teasing," I say, tweaking a nipple playfully.

There are long hours spent talking in front of the fire, eating his tremendously satisfying elven food, dozing in his magnificently soft bed. But my favorite part is drifting off to sleep with him reading to me aloud. He reads to me from memory, any book I can name. If he hasn't read it, the trees provide it to him. It's too strange, magical, and romantic that I never want this life to end.

And still, in the back of my mind, I know, someday it will.

One morning I awaken to El drawing designs on my back with his finger.

I smile and tell him he's giving me chills.

"Can you guess what I'm writing?"

"Is it English?"

"No," he says. "I'm asking you a question in Elvish."

"If it's not Tolkien Elvish, then I'm lost."

I wait for him to dismiss the author's invented language, but he doesn't.

"I'm asking you if you'd like to venture outside to find a Christmas tree?"

Rolling over to face him, I tell him I have no desire to cut down one of the trees from the Elder Woods.

"No," he says. "Not one of mine. I mean, would you like to finish your date to the farm with me?"

I don't know how he does it, but he just made me fall in love with him all over again.

"What made you want to ask me that?"

He smiles wide. "Because it's Christmas Eve."

Donning our elven winter cloaks—and I'm surprised to see that El owns pants and a shirt—we hold hands and prepare to leave our home in search of holiday cheer to make the space even more festive.

To our shock and surprise, two figures in hoods step inside the hovel, out of the cold.

I shriek, and El pulls me into his side.

When the two figures lower their hoods, the two familiar faces look back at me and smile serenely.

I think I might pass out.

"Reba? Deacon?"

I can't believe my eyes.

"What are you two doing here?"

Reba and Deacon exchange knowing looks.

"I guess I'd better explain," Reba starts.

Eldrin turns to me, looking sheepish.

"You know them?" I ask him.

He looks from me to Reba. "I think you should tell her."

"What is going on?" I insist. "Somebody better start explaining!"

Reba looks at Deacon, and he glances back in both apprehension and excitement.

I take in the full vision of my best friend and her fiancé and the stunning clothes they're wearing. Reba wears a royal blue coat covered in glittering precious stones, with a collar and cuffs of ermine. Her braids crown her head in an unearthly design I can't even describe, and it too glitters with tiny gemstones that have the effect of freshly fallen snow. Her boots are leather and lace up the front. Deacon is similarly dressed and holds a bag in his hand.

"We came bearing gifts. It's Christmas Eve."

Deacon says this as if that clears everything up.

"I'll explain everything. But first some tea, and a seat by the fire," Reba says.

Chapter Twelve

ELDRIN

Clara sits with her hands covering her cheeks as she listens. While I knew that Reba and Deacon were half-elves condemned to live as full humans for no reason other than they were not fully elves, I'm learning more now. I didn't know they were secret underground messengers between the human and the Elven worlds. And they've come with shocking news.

What Reba explains is this:

After I left the North Pole five years ago, the Uncommon and Common elves united and began to revolt.

Nicholas was working them too hard. They toiled endlessly; they had no time for family, no time for friends. No time for love or joy of any kind.

Nicholas didn't care. He had a workforce of thousands who were practically immortal. Or, at least, who would outlast him. He would live about a hundred more years and already had dozens of children who were suitable candidates to be the heir to the sleigh one day.

"Well, eventually, the elves had had enough, and they unionized. They floated Santa out on an iceberg along with his wife and said adios," Reba says, miming a wave goodbye with her hand. "Then today, they voted for a new Nicholas."

She looks right at me as if she's preparing herself for the next bit of information. She draws in a deep breath. "They voted for you, El. They want you to be the next Nicholas."

Clara has many questions, surprising no one.

"You're a part of all this? Why didn't you tell me?"

"It was never the right time to tell you. Would you have believed me if you had not experienced...all of this?" Reba gestures around the room as if the very air is magic.

Clara warily shakes her head no.

Reba goes on. "So when I heard our friend here was exiled for his little obsession, and I found out why, I came looking for you, Clara."

"You knew this entire time? That's why we're friends?" I don't like the scared note in Clara's voice, and I slide my arm around her and pull her back into my side.

"Have you wondered why I haven't aged in the five years since we met?" Reba asks.

Clara ignores this question. "But if you decided to help him, why did you send me on all those dates?"

Deacon wheezes, stirring his tea.

"You have something to say over there, Chuckles?" Clara barks, and I have to stifle a laugh because I know she's frustrated and wants answers. I don't blame her.

Deacon finally answers. "She was matching you with the worst of the worst to drive you to El eventually. Sooner or later, you would get mopey and end up at the tree farm to cheer you up with some holiday fun. All you needed was a little push."

"I have to take a walk. I need some air."

Chapter Thirteen

Clara

"I don't understand why you are so upset," El tells me when we transition to the outdoors. I'm pacing back and forth in the snow.

I whirl around to face El.

"Clara, your cheeks are flushed with cold. I want to pick you up and take you back to the fire, but I feel like you need to say something to me first."

Nodding, I reply, "I'm upset. My roommate has been orchestrating my life for years, just to lead me to you. None of this was my choice. Do you understand how manipulated I feel?"

"Very well. You may leave. You have a choice."

"I don't want to leave you."

Eldrin laughs, and It's infuriating.

"I'm still so mad at them!"

"You have five minutes to get over it because if you agree

to accompany me, I have half a billion presents to deliver before midnight."

I take the full five minutes and trudge through the snow, muttering and doing the math in my head.

Just then, we are joined outside by Reba and Deacon.

"And in case you had any doubts about your role in all of this, Nicholas gets to choose his mate. Elven, human, or hybrid, his lifemate is granted the same long life as the Nicholas. So, there's that, if that helps the two of you make a decision," Reba announces.

Looking up at Eldrin, I ask him, "Is this what you want? You want to be freaking Santa Claus?"

He's choosing his words carefully, trying not to influence me. It's adorable, mainly because I came here, to these woods, under the influence of several individuals.

"I never envisioned myself as Nicholas. My fellow elves have done me an enormous honor. I can't say I want it or don't want it."

Turning back to Reba, I still feel the heaviness in my heart that I've been living with a half-elf this entire time and didn't know it.

"I feel as though I've been treated like a puppet on a string. I wish you would have just told me when you met me," I tell her.

Tears shine in my best friend's eyes.

"I'm sorry, Clara. That I never told you the truth was my biggest regret in all of this. I'm so sorry. It's just that humans don't usually react well to being told that magical elves are real."

I cock my head and give my friend a small smile. "Have you seen my Legolas collection?"

Reba sighs heavily. "I should've trusted you with the truth."

"And I understand why you didn't," I say. I wrap my

friend in a hug. We still have a lot to talk about, but I'm not going to lose my friend over it.

Also, time is ticking.

Pulling away from the hug, I turn to look up at Eldrin. He clutches me to him possessively.

He slants his face down, so his eyes are at the same level as mine. "What's it going to be?"

El knows he's got me. He knows that I can't go back to my humdrum life after that. I want a life with him and with my friends, whatever that looks like. I can't be mad forever, and I don't have any more time to think it over before billions of kids are due some gifts under their trees.

Okay, fine. I'm over it. Because there's nothing I love more than my giant elf other than Christmas.

A long life with both?

I take his hand in mine and say, "Let's go deliver some presents."

Epilogue

THE NORTH POLE

Ten years later

Eldrin

My wife skates up next to me on the rink and sees me eyeing my children's hideous outfits.

"You may not consent to me dressing you as a department store Christmas elf, but our children have no choice. Let me have this," she says to me. And how can I refuse?

It's Christmas Day, my day off. My family has their heart set on ice skating, a popular tradition in North Pole Village.

Today, four pairs of striped legs are whirling and twirling around the ice pond with me, our friends, and my Queen of Christmas. The terrible striped stockings on our half-elf children were all Clara's doing.

"Be sure they're dressed in proper elven garb for Christmas dinner," I grumble. Clara squeezes my backside before skating off again.

My Clara has adapted to live at the North Pole even better than I expected, now that my exile is over. Four children are a handful when you're also Santa Claus all year round. Still, we do pretty well with the help of, well, literally thousands of happy elves.

Reba and Deacon are a help, too. At the moment, both of them are out on the ice, pulling our smallest ones along bit by bit as their little legs learn how to maneuver. Our two oldest children are teaching their mother how to spin, and I can hear Clara marveling at their abilities on the ice.

It was pure joy to watch my wife stand in awe at how early our little ones learned how to walk and talk in the beginning. She's never lost her sense of wonder at our magical world, and seeing all of this through her eyes has made my role as Nicholas that much sweeter.

Fortunately, Sugar, Plum, Candy, and Winter did not arrive as twins. Each of them was born a year apart. The conception efficiency trait doesn't work with a human partner. Thank gods.

I exit the rink to fetch my wife some hot cocoa. When I turn from the eternally-flowing hot coca fountain, I hear a small, hesitant voice.

"Sir? I mean...Nicholas?"

I look down, and it's the mother of one of Plum's friends addressing me, wringing her hands. Why the others feel scared to address me as one of their own is totally to blame on the previous Nicholas.

"Yes, hello," I reply.

"I just wanted to say, the North Pole and Santa's Workshop is so much happier now with you in charge," she says.

Out of the corner of my eye, I see my wife leaving the ice, heading our way.

"Oh, that's so kind of you. Thank you for saying so," I say to the grateful young mother.

I can successfully deliver gifts to billions of children in one night. Yet, I can't escape small talk with people who are still traumatized by the old man. I just can't get away from it.

None of the credit for this place being a happier environment to live and work in goes to me. Under my rule, the Common elves chose to continue making toys in the workshop. The Uncommon elves voted to dissolve the entire Naughty or Nice list and any and all surveillance of children. This move, I wholeheartedly agreed with. All children get presents now, no matter what. And the Uncommon Elves now use their powers of invisibility to help me deliver gifts. They serve as a sort of guardian angel corps for the rest of the year.

Plum's friend's mother and I discuss some of the finer points of some of the more recent changes at the factories. Soon, I feel my Clara slipping her arm around my waist. "I'm sorry to interrupt, but I think I have to show you the new toy in the workshop, El," she says.

I know that voice. She's jealous.

Plum's friend's mother bats her eyelashes and exchanges pleasantries with my wife before turning and scuttling away.

Moments later, the two of us are locked inside the empty workshop.

I can't help but tease my jealous wife. "Darling, won't the children wonder where we are?"

Clara looks back at me over her shoulder while she leads me down an aisle of workstations by the hand, her skates clanking together in the other hand. She was in such a hurry when she saw me talking to Plum's friend's mother that she didn't even have time to put her skates away.

"Reba and Deacon are taking them for the rest of the afternoon."

I smile wickedly. "Oh, you mean they aren't going to Plum's friend's house?"

Clara arches an eyebrow.

I'm in trouble.

Because it is the day after Christmas, and all toymakers have the next month off, so no elf has any reason to be here but me and my queen.

Hoisting my Clara up on a worktable, I plant myself between her knees. "What did you have to show me, my love?"

Clara's eyes flash as she hands me a box. "Open it. Your present."

Inside the box is an array of new devices—the sort of toys that do not belong anywhere near Santa's workshop.

"Human, how dare you?"

She smirks. "How dare you let that woman flirt with you when I take my eyes off you for five minutes."

"Clara."

"El."

"How often do I have to explain to you you're the only one for me, for the next several centuries? At least."

Clara runs her hand over my hardening length and bites her lip. "I guess you'll have to just pound it into me until I get it."

My arousal flares at her filthy words, and in seconds I have her bent over the worktable, and her skirt flipped up over her back.

I playfully slap one full, round cheek, then tug her candy-cane-printed panties to the side. Sliding one finger into her slick heat, I blithely use my free hand to remove one of the toys from the box. She pushes back against my finger, her body demanding an in-and-out motion.

"Not just yet," I scold her.

After examining the toy, I gently run the smooth, metallic tip through her wetness.

Clara gasps. "Is that...?"

"You said you would be a good girl. But you got jealous, and now you have to be punished."

She moans, turning to look at me over her shoulder. "You're the one who was flirting," she seethes. "You can't turn the tables on me."

Slowly, I lean over her and whisper into her hair. "But I can keep you turned over this table until I'm finished."

I love these games we play. But I've had enough of these panties, and I rip them to shreds with satisfaction. Massaging Clara's cheeks, I spread her wide. The toy, glistening with her essence, slips inside her quickly. I watch my queen for any discomfort.

"Oh god," she breathes.

"Tell me if it hurts. We've not done this before, and I want to make sure—"

"It's good. Oh my god, it's so fucking good. I need you, too. I need you right now."

My cock slides right into her heat, and the feeling of home and all good things floods my soul. Her snug little cunt was built for me. I reach around to tease her clit while I push in.

"Product review?"

With one thrust, she gasps and then exhales. "Good. Comfortable. Oh god. So full. So fucking full with your cock at the same time... it's...."

Another thrust. "And your overall rating?"

Clara looks back and me and bites her lip. "Five stars."

Thrust. "And?"

She moans and manages to say, "Would use again."

Thrust. "Anything else?"

"Would recommend. Oh my god, El!" My fingers command her sweet, tight little clit to rocket my queen into oblivion. Her orgasm rattles the windows of the workshop, and my own release, I fear, might blow the doors off.

They'll hear us outside!" she hisses.

True. It's not like the little hovel in the woods, where no one was around.

I really should learn to be quieter. On the other hand, it's fucking Santa Claus, bitch. I may be a benevolent ruler, but I'll fuck my queen as loudly as I want.

I wouldn't want to live any other way.

We have a literal village looking after our children. We would be happy in the hovel in the woods, but we wouldn't have any sort of community. And the old Nick would still be in charge.

This life is tons of responsibility. Parenting, on top of it, is madness.

I flip my wife over and lay with her on my chest, right on top of the worktable where the Fisher-Price toys are made.

The two of us cling to each other, still trembling through the aftershocks of our releases. "Did you have a good Christmas, El?"

She already knows the answer to that. Every Christmas Day is wonderful because it's my day off, and I get to spend it with her and the children.

The entire month of January is spent celebrating and relaxing for everyone who works in the North Pole Village.

"You know I did," I tell her, kissing the top of her damp, warm head. Out of breath, I inhale her scent into my lungs, and it settles me down. She has that way about her.

She murmurs, "I forgot to give you one gift. I thought you could wear it tonight. After the kids are asleep, of course."

Clara hops down and fetches a small box from under the worktable.

I sit up and open the second box of the afternoon. This time, I'm looking at my old leather kilt. "Sweetheart. This is thoughtful, and I don't know how you found this. But as you know, it no longer fits me." I pat myself around the slight spare tire I've developed since settling down with my Clara.

My wife rubs at my love handles and informs me that one of the more discreet toy makers in the clothing department had the kilt let out a few inches.

"So, will you wear it for me? Please?"

Chuckling, I ask, "Do I have a choice?"

"Sure," Clara answers. "You can choose to try it out now or listen to me ask you again and again for a millennium."

She doesn't know that receiving her questions for a millennium gives me life.

She may tease me that I'm stuck with a human for what seems like an eternity. But the truth is, she was the one who kidnapped my heart from the very beginning. And I never want to escape.

THE END

A Filthy Dirty Christmas

Welcome to a filthy dirty Christmas! Forget sugar and spice and everything nice … this year we want to show off our naughty side. Taboo, dangerous, and over-the-top, we're bringing you everything you were too scared to ask Santa for.

**Don't worry, loves, these are still packed with the heroes you crave and the HEA's you deserve!

VCard for Christmas by Hope Ford
    XL Candy Cane by Frankie Love
    Knotty or Nice by Ines Johnson
    Stalk and Stuff Her by Jenna Rose
    On His Naughty List by Kat Baxter
    Unwrapping His Package by Fiona Davenport
    Santa's Dirty Secret by Lana Dash
    Step-Santa by Logan Chance
    We Three Kings by Alice May Ball
    Santa Claus is Coming by Jane Fox
    Secret Santa by Mayra Statham
    SILF (Santa I'd Like to F*) by Lana Love
    Santa's Baby by Chloe Maine

Kiss My Tinsel by Melissa Schroeder
Decking Her Halls by Elisa Leigh
Wanna Scrooge? By Lily Nicole
Father Christmas by Margot Scott
The Christmas Virgin by Tory Baker
Capturing Christmas by Jagger Cole
Oooo Holy Night by Dani Wyatt
Sleigh My Name by Tarin Lex
Elf-napped by Abby Knox
Naughty Little Elf by Nichole Rose
Ringing His Bells by Flora Ferrari
Coming Down His Chimney by Shaw Hart and Cameron Hart

About the Author

Abby Knox writes feel-good, high-heat romance that she herself would want to read. Readers have described her stories as quirky, sexy, adorable, and hilarious. All of that adds up to Abby's overall goal in life: to be kind and to have fun!

Abby's favorite tropes include: Forced proximity, opposites attract, grumpy/sunshine, age gap, boss/employee, fated mates/insta-love, and more. Abby is heavily influenced by Buffy the Vampire Slayer, Gilmore Girls, and LOST. But don't worry, she won't ever make you suffer like Luke & Lorelai.

If any or all of that connects with you, then you came to the right place.

To find me on social media or to join my newsletter, please visit my website at authorabbyknox.com

Paradise Passions
Babymoon
(insta-lust, breeding)
Honeymoon Hideout
(childhood/celebrity crush)

Homemade Heat
Judge Me
(age gap)
Cake Walk
(age gap, dad's best friend)
Hand-Tossed
(boss/employee)
Chef's Kiss
(boss/employee. Hero steals the bride)
Bite Me
(age gap)

Crow Bar Brute Squad
Party Foul
(fake relationship)
Dirty Martini
(Older woman billionaire/younger man)
Whiskey Sour
(enemies to lovers)

And plenty more on my website authorabbyknox.com